what time is it?

IT'S DUFFY TIME!

Audrey & Don Wood

THE BLUE SKY PRESS

An Imprint of Scholastic Inc. • *New York*

THE BLUE SKY PRESS

Text copyright © 2012 by Audrey Wood

Illustrations copyright © 2012 by Don Wood

Library of Congress catalog card number 2012006174

ISBN 978-0-545-22089-7

10 9 8 7 6 5 4 3 2 1   12 13 14 15 16

Printed in Singapore   46

First printing, October 2012

Duffy dedicates this book to his veterinarian,
Dr. Alan Nagakura

OH NO!
Duffy overslept!
The air smells like breakfast.

Duffy races into the kitchen
and asks for a bite to eat.

"Not yet," his mistress says.
"It's time to go out and potty."
So Duffy does.

Waiting at the door
in the warm sunshine makes
Duffy sleepy, so he takes his
BEFORE BREAKFAST nap.

Breakfast at last! Duffy gobbles every bite.
He even licks the floor to make sure
he doesn't leave a crumb.

Because his tummy feels round and full,
Duffy knows it's time for his
AFTER BREAKFAST nap.

"Wake up, Duffy!" his mistress calls.
"We've got business to do.
 Where's your pirate hat?"

The line at the bank
is long, but at least
Duffy gets a
biscuit.

On the ride back
Duffy is exhausted.
He curls up for his
LATE MORNING nap.

It is good to be home. Duffy can't resist taking a quick MID-DAY nap in his comfy chair. The MID-DAY nap goes so well,

Duffy sleeps straight through
into his EARLY AFTERNOON nap.
A long nap makes for the best dreams.

"Duffeeeey!" a voice calls. His best friend is home

from school, and that means it's . . . Duffy time!

He wants to play longer,
but his best friend has
homework to do.
Duffy helps.

Something good is cooking in the kitchen.
Duffy asks for a nibble, but his food isn't ready,
so he takes his BEFORE DINNER nap, in a place
where no one will forget to feed him.

After dinner, the family goes
for a walk in the park.

Duffy enjoys sniffing trees
and saying hello to his friends.

OH NO!
Back at home, the master has stolen
Duffy's comfy chair, but he squeezes in
his EARLY EVENING nap anyway.

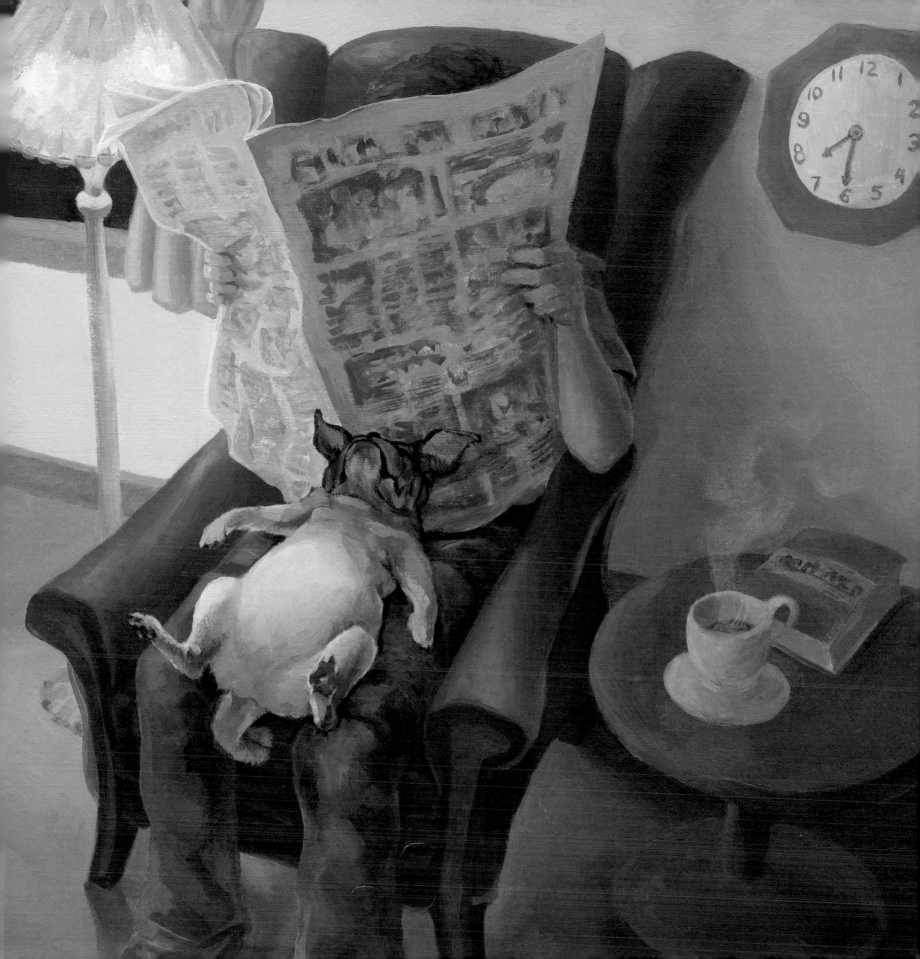

"Time to get ready for bed,"
his best friend calls.
Just for fun they dress in
matching pajamas.

There's nothing better than having your
best friend read you a good book at bedtime.
Duffy snuggles down and sighs with pleasure.
He doesn't feel sleepy at all.

E   Wood, Audrey.   1
Wood
         It's Duffy time!

         1699

DATE			
JAN 1 2 2016 //x/2/5			
OCT 3 1 2019 /8×/1/9			
MAR 1 7 2020 /8×/1/9			

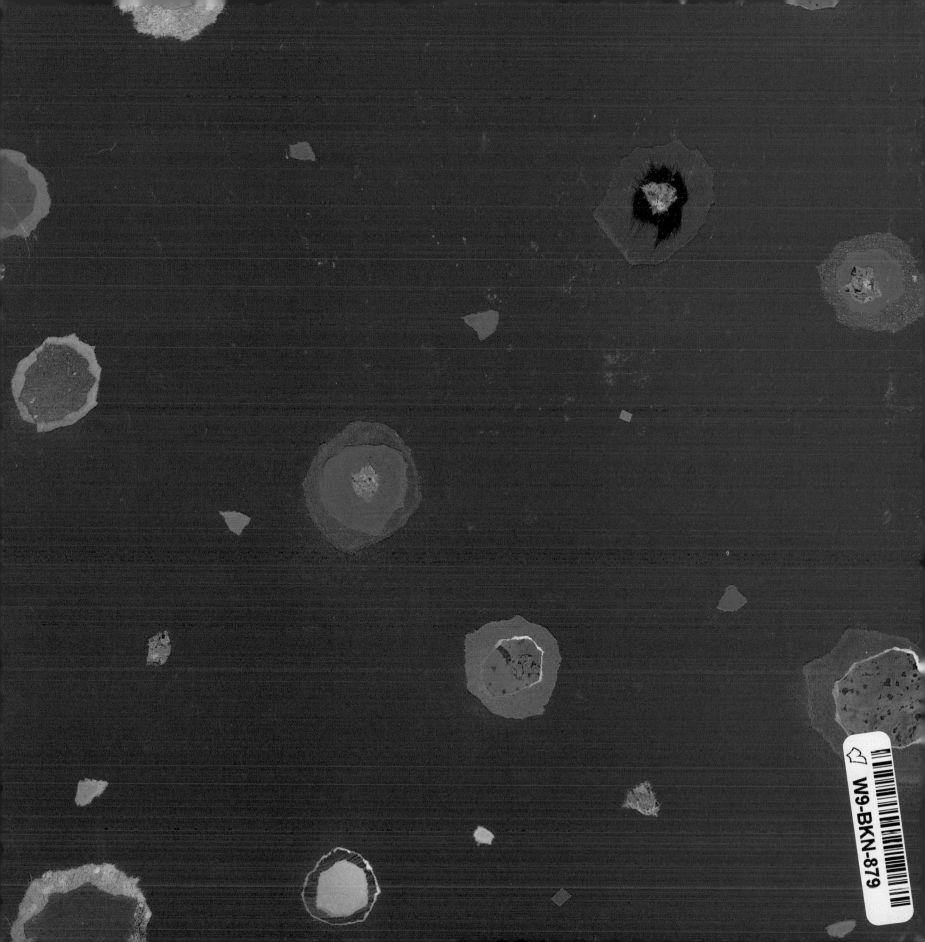

To Dr. Robert Wilkinson who is frequently humerus.

And to my boney wife.

Dem Bones is one of the most well-known and loved African American spirituals. A song about resurrection, Dem Bones was probably first sung in church and at revival meetings as long as two hundred years ago. As with most spirituals, there is an African music influence in the song's repetitive structure and humor. Passed on by word of mouth for generations, the song has many versions. Today the song is usually sung by children as a way to learn anatomy, rhyme and language.

Designed by Cathleen O'Brien
Original text type designed by Lilly Lee
Printed in Hong Kong
The illustrations in this book were rendered in paper collage,
created with papers from all over the world.

Library of Congress Information
Dem bones/illustrated by Bob Barner.
  p.cm
  ISBN 0-8118-0827-0
  1. Human skeleton—Juvenile literature. 2. Bones—Juvenile
literature. [1. Skeleton. 2. Bones.] I. Barner, Bob.
QM101.D79 1995
611'.71—dc20
                                               95-29
                                               CIP
                                               AC

Distributed in Canada by Raincoast Books
8680 Cambie Street
Vancouver B.C. V6P 6M9

Distributed in Australia and New Zealand
by CIS Cardigan Street
245-249 Cardigan Street, Carlton 3053 Australia

10 9 8 7 6 5 4 3 2

Chronicle Books
85 Second Street
San Francisco, CA 94105

Web Site: www.chronbooks.com

Dem Bones

Bob Barner

chronicle books · san francisco

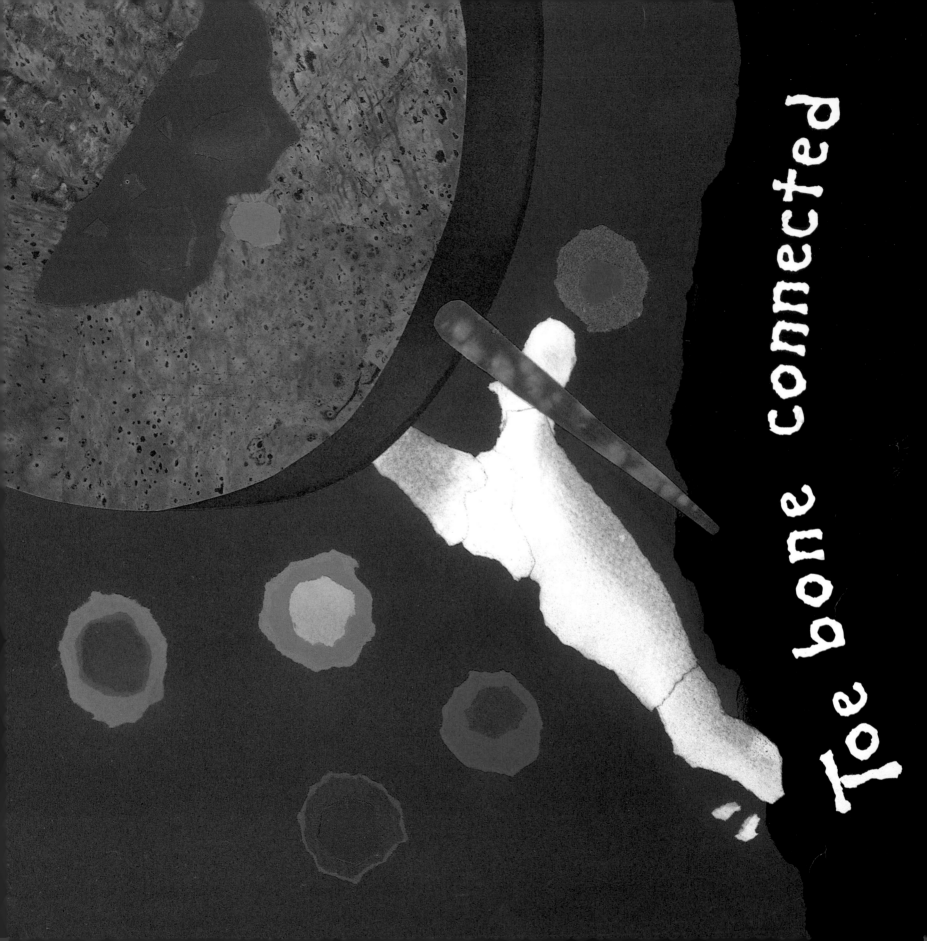

Toe bone connected

to da foot bone.

FOOT BONE

The foot bones are
the basement of your
skeleton. The twenty-
two bones in your
foot support the
entire weight of your
body. A built-in arch
helps absorb shock
when you walk,
run or jump.

ANKLE BONE

Without ankle bones
you wouldn't be able
to lift your feet when
you walk. Because the
ankle bone swivels, it
allows the foot to flex
so you can climb
stairs, run or dance.

Foot
bone connected to
da ankle bone.

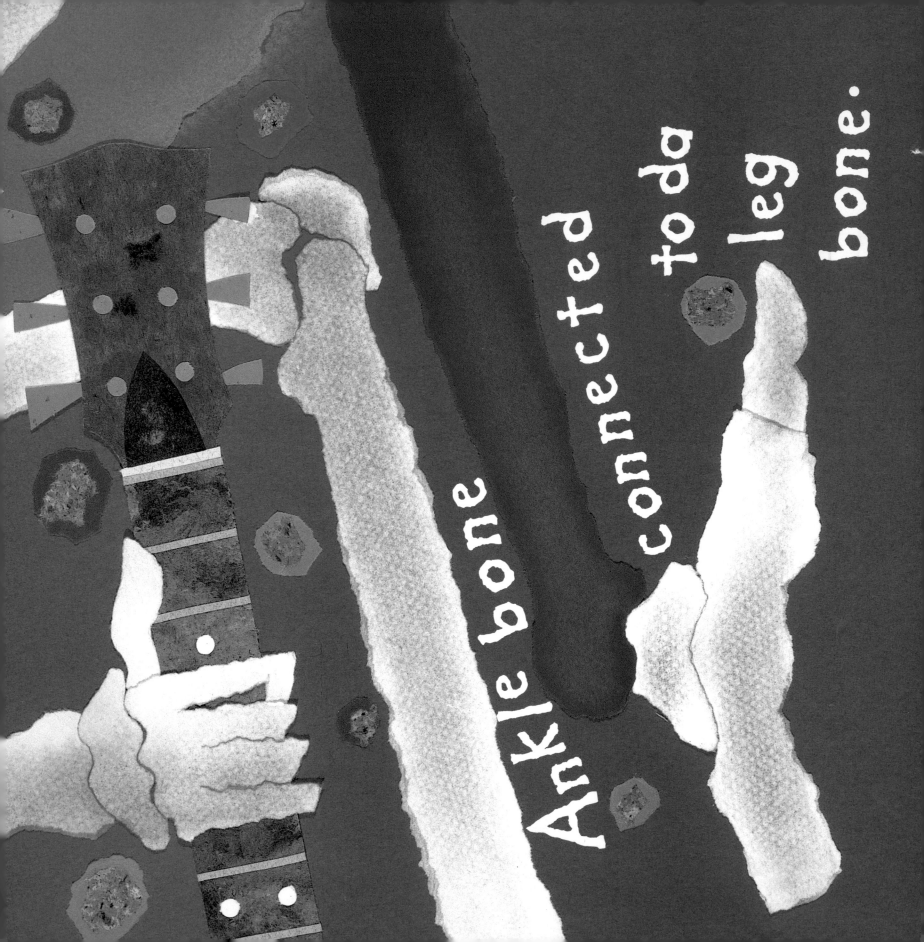

Ankle bone connected to da leg bone.

LEG BONE

The leg bone is actually two bones, the tibia and the fibula. The fibula, the smaller of the two, is located on the little toe side of your leg. You can feel the tibia at the front of your lower leg. It's the one that really hurts if you get kicked in the shin!

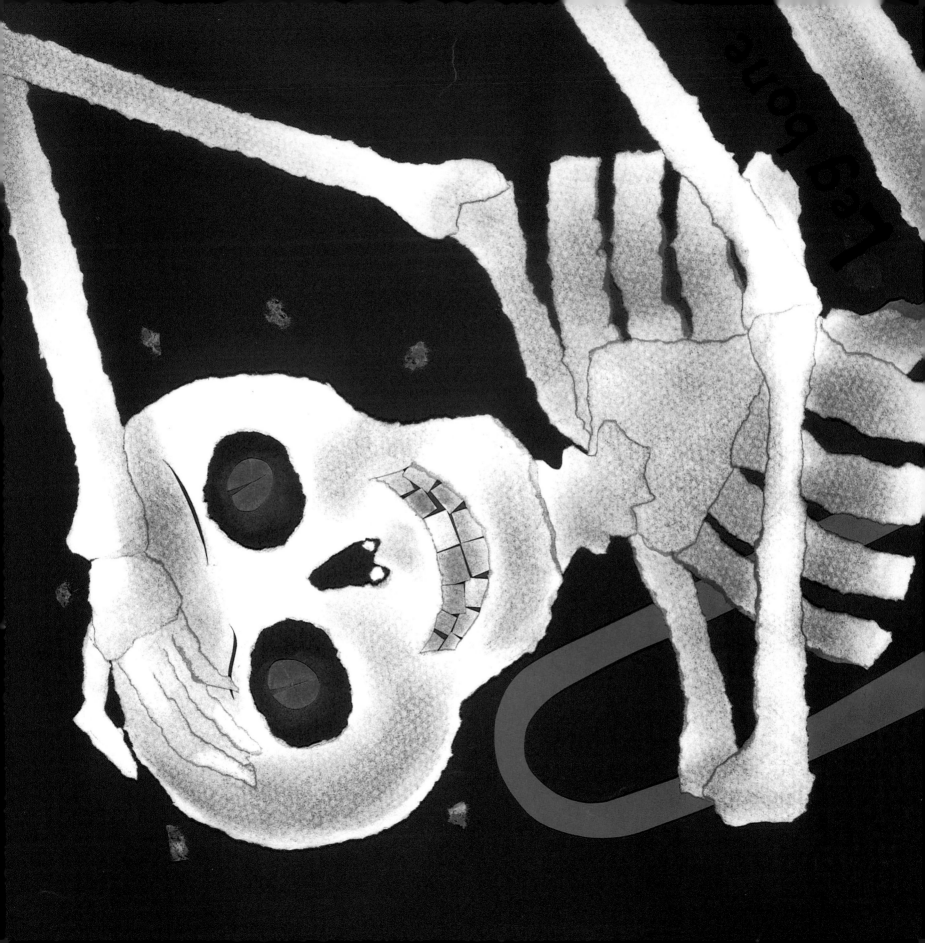

KNEE BONE

The knee bone (also known as the kneecap or patella) covers and protects the knee joint. The knee joint works like a hinge on a door so you can kick, jump, squat and dance.

connected to a knee bone.

THIGH BONE

The thigh bone, or femur, is the longest and heaviest bone in your body. The top of the femur has a ball joint that moves within a socket in the pelvis.

Knee bone

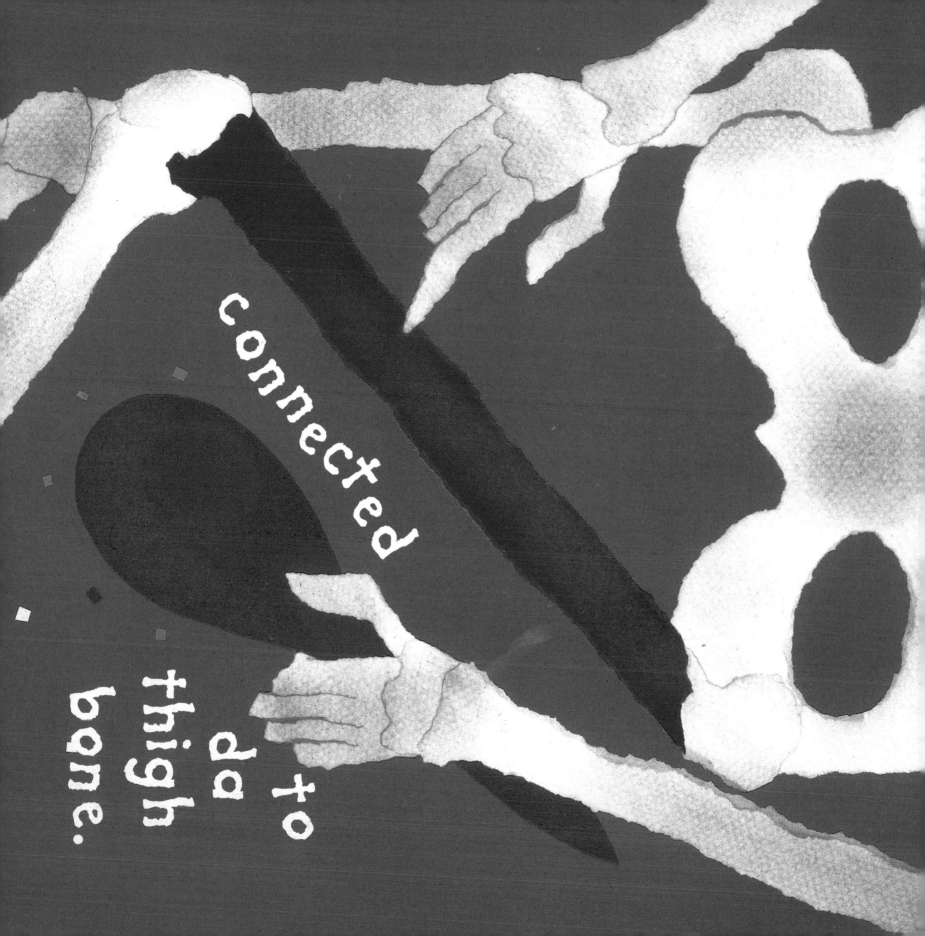

HIP BONE

The hip bone, or pelvis, is made up of six bones. Sockets in the pelvis hold the ball joints at the top of the thigh bones. The biggest difference between the male and female skeleton is in the hip bones. The female hip bone is wider and lighter.

Thigh bone connected to da hip bone.

Hip bone connected to

BACKBONE

You couldn't stand up straight without your backbone! The backbone, or spinal column, is made up of twenty-four vertebrae. The last four bones in your backbone form the coccyx, the remnant of a tail! The most important job of the backbone is to protect your spinal cord.

da back bone.

SHOULDER BONE

Actually made up of a team of three bones: the clavicle, scapula and the top of the humerus, the shoulder bone is the most frequently broken bone among children. The humerus rotates in a ball and socket joint so you can move your arms around.

Back bone connected

NECK BONE

The neck bone is a continuation of the backbone or spine. It is made up of seven vertebrae called cervical vertebrae. These seven bones in your neck rotate so you can turn your head from side to side, nod yes or no and wiggle your head in time to music.

Shoulder bone connected to da neck bone.

HEAD BONE

The head bone, or skull, is like a box that grows. The skull, which is made up of twenty-nine bones, is about 50% of adult size at birth and continues to grow quickly during the first year of life. Most importantly, the skull protects your brain when you stand on your head!

Neck bone connected

to do head bone.

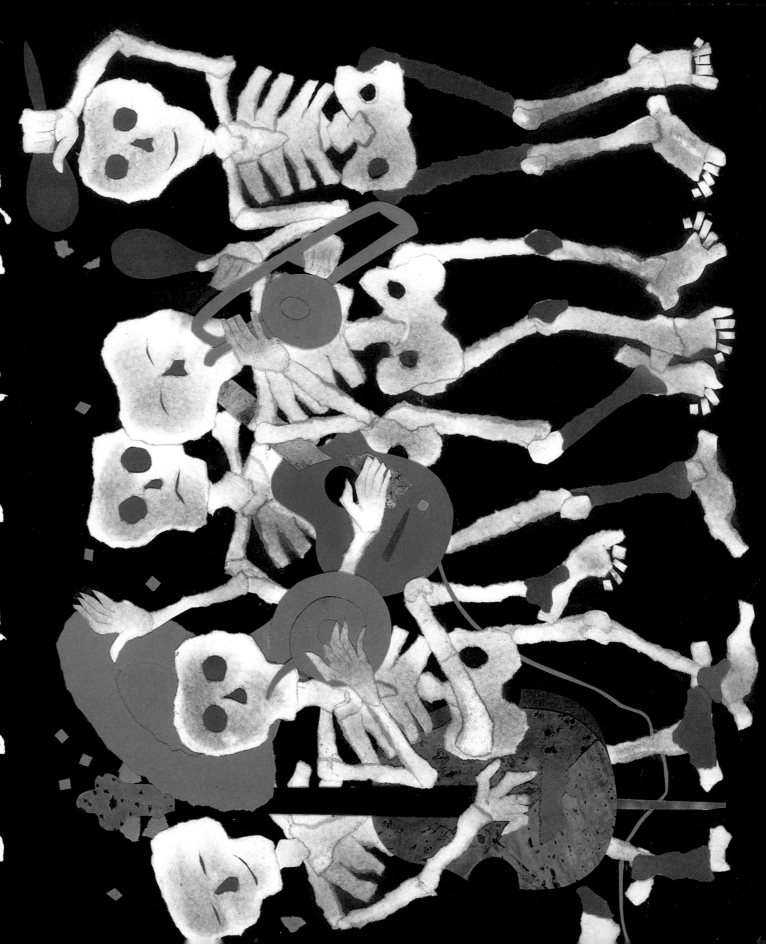

Dem Bones, Dem Bones, Dem Dry Bones
Dem Bones, Dem Bones, Dem Dry Bones

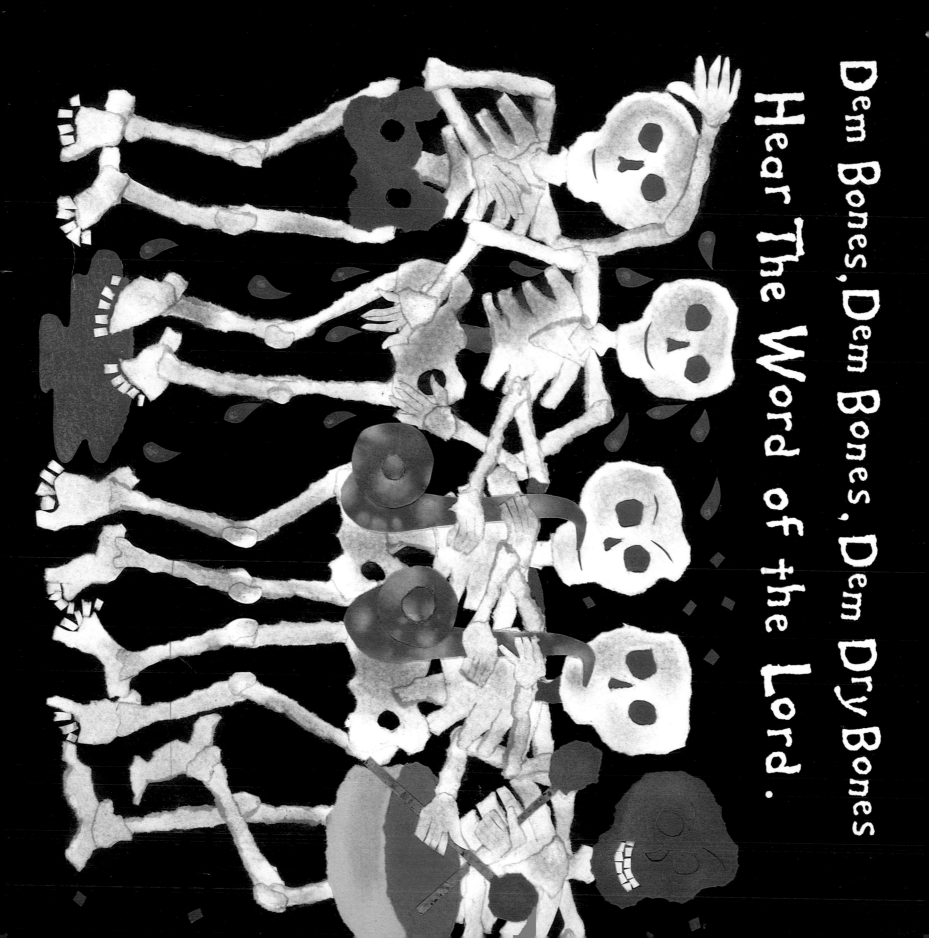

Dem Bones, Dem Bones, Dem Dry Bones

Hear The Word of the Lord.

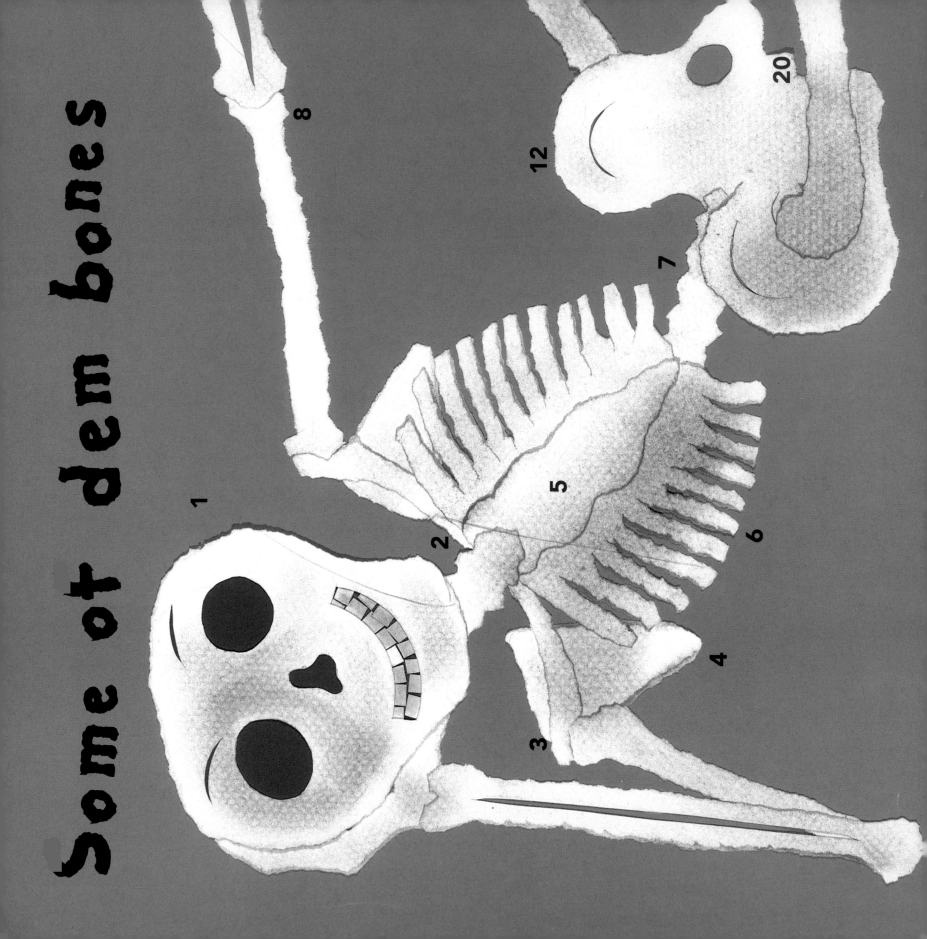

When we are born we have about 450 bones, but when we reach adulthood we only have 206. This is because many of the bones, like those in the skull, grow together. This list includes just some of those 206 bones.

1. Skull (Head Bone)
2. Neck Vertebrae (Neck Bone)
3. Clavicle
4. Scapula
5. Sternum
6. Ribs
7. Lumbar Vertebrae (Backbone)
8. Humerus
9. Ulna
10. Radius
11. Phalanges (Finger Bones)
12. Pelvis (Hip Bone)
13. Femur (Thigh Bone)
14. Patella (Knee Bone)
15. Tibia (Leg Bone)
16. Fibula (Leg Bone)
17. Tarsals (Ankle Bone)
18. Metatarsals (Foot Bones)
19. Phalanges (Toe Bones)
20. Coccyx

9

10

11

13

14

15

16

17

18

19

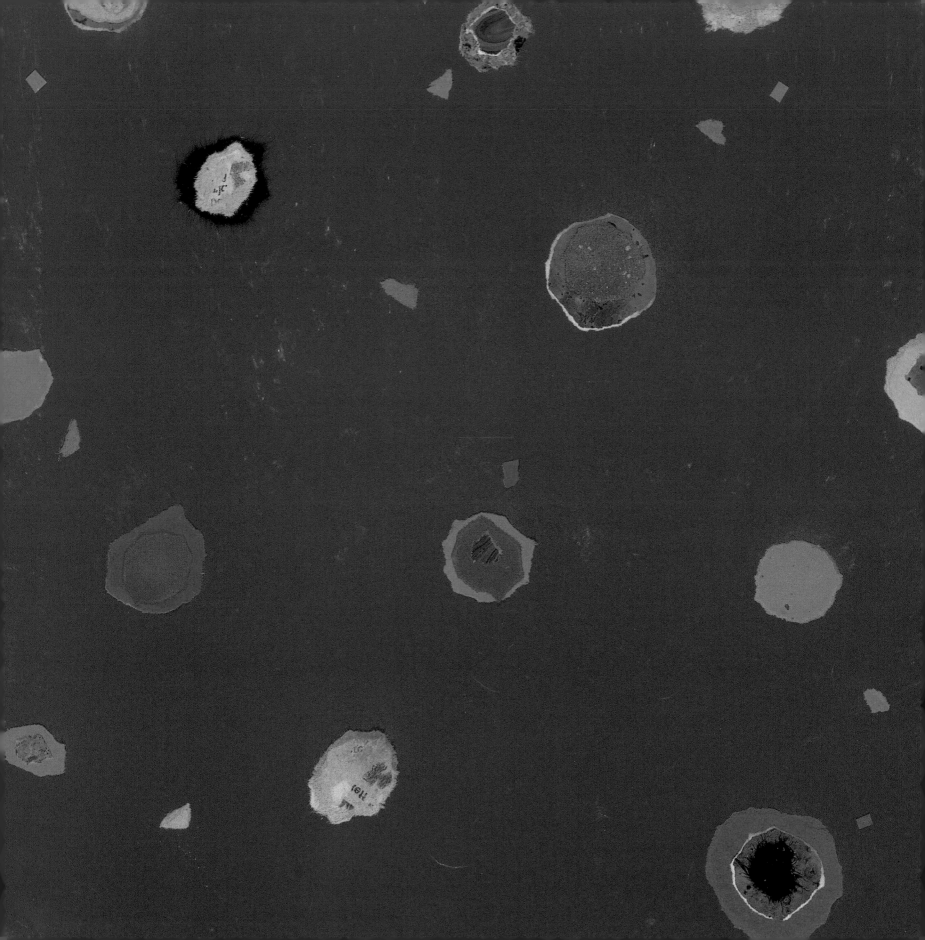